THE EMPEROR'S NEW CLOTHES
By Hans Christian Andersen
Translated from the original Danish text by Marlee Alex
Illustrated by Héléne Desputeaux
Published by Scandinavia Publishing House,
Nørregade 32, DK-1165 Copenhagen; Denmark
Text:©Copyright 1984 Scandinavia Publishing House
Artwork:©Copyright 1984 Héléne Desputeaux and
Scandinavia Publishing House
Printed in Italy

ISBN 0 8317-2736-5

The Emperor's New Clothes

Hans Christian Andersen
Illustrated by Héléne Desputeaux

GALLERY BOOKS
An Imprint of W. H. Smith Publishers Inc.
112 Madison Avenue
New York City 10016

Once upon a time there lived an Emperor who was so very fond of beautiful new clothes that he spent all his money to be well dressed. He wasn't interested in his soldiers, nor in going to the theatre, nor in riding in the great parks, unless it was to show off his new clothes. He had an outfit for every hour of the day, and just like the old saying: "the King is in his council chambers," people would say about the Emperor: "he is in his dressing room."

In the great city where he lived, there was a lot of festivity. Every day many travelling tradesmen came to town. One day two rogues arrived. They pretended to be weavers and told everyone that they knew how to weave the loveliest cloth that could be imagined. They said that not only were the colours and designs unusually beautiful, but that the clothes made from the cloth had a remarkable quality: they became invisible for any person who wasn't qualified for his position, or who was unforgivably foolish.

"How nice," thought the Emperor. "By wearing these clothes, I will recognize which men in my kingdom are not fit for their jobs. I will be able to tell the wise from the foolish. Yes, these clothes must be woven for me immediately!" He gave the two rogues a lot of money so that they could begin their work.

They set up two chairs before a loom and pretended to be working, but there was absolutely nothing on the loom. From distant countries they ordered the finest silk and the purest gold fibres which they put in their own bag for themselves. For the Emperor they continued working on the empty loom. They worked on and on until very late every night.

"It's about time I find out how soon my clothes will be ready!" thought the Emperor. However, he was a bit anxious when he thought about the fact that the person who was foolish or who wasn't clever couldn't see them.

Now, he probably didn't think he had anything to fear himself, but he could just as well send someone else first to see how it was going. All the people in the whole town knew of the unusual power of the clothes, and they were all greedy enough to want to see how foolish their neighbours were.

"I will send my old, honest Prime Minister to the weavers!" thought the Emperor. "For he is quite intelligent, and no-one is more qualified for his position than he is!" So the quaint old man went to the workroom where the two cheats sat weaving at the empty loom. "Bless my soul!" thought the old man; and his eyes nearly popped out of their sockets. "I can't see anything!" But he didn't say it out loud.
The swindlers asked him to step closer. "Isn't it a marvellous design? Aren't these colours lovely?" they asked, and they pointed at the empty loom. The poor old Prime Minister opened his eyes as wide as he could, but he couldn't see anything, for there was nothing to see. "Good heavens!" he thought, "am I a fool? I would never have believed it, and nobody must know! Could it be that I am not fit for my job? No, it will never ever do for me to say that I cannot see the clothes!"

"Well, what do you think of it?" asked one of the crooks as he pretended to weave. "Oh, it's stunning! It's just exquisite!" said the old man as he peered through his spectacles. "This design, and those colours! Yes, I will tell the Emperor that it will please him very much indeed."

"Well, that's nice to hear!" said both weavers, and then they described the colours and the intricate pattern in detail. The old man listened well, so that he could describe it when he reported to the Emperor. And he did just that!

11

Now the rogues wanted more money, more silk and more gold fibres which they said they needed for the weaving. They put it all into their own pockets so that not a thread of it appeared on the loom, and they continued as before to weave on the empty loom. The Emperor soon sent another of his old and trusted advisers over to see how the weaving was going, and to find out if the clothes would be finished soon. The old man experienced the same thing as the Prime Minister had. He looked and looked, but as there was nothing to see, he didn't see anything.

"Now isn't this a beautiful piece of cloth?" asked both the swindlers as they pretended to display it and as they described the lovely pattern that wasn't there.

"I am certainly no fool!" thought the man, "is it then my job I'm not fit for? That's ridiculous! People will laugh; I must not let anyone know!" And so he praised the cloth he couldn't see and reassured them that he was pleased with the fine texture and the lovely design. "Yes, it is most exquisite!" he reported to the Emperor.

13

14

All over town people were talking about the magnificent cloth.

At length the Emperor himself wished to see it while it was still on the loom. Along with a large assembly of distinguished men (among which were the Prime Minister and the Advisor) he went directly to the two swindlers who were now weaving frantically without thread.

"Isn't it magnificent?" asked both of the honest, old men who had been there before. "Will Your Majesty be pleased to look here? Such a design! What colours!" they exclaimed as they pointed at the empty loom, pretending that all the others could see the cloth just like them.

"What is this?" thought the Emperor. "I don't see a thing. This is frightful! Am I a fool? Am I not fit to be the Emperor? This is the most dreadful thing that could ever happen to me." "Oh, they are very beautiful!" said the Emperor aloud, "they have my highest approval." And he nodded in satisfaction as he studied the empty loom. He wouldn't admit that he couldn't see anything.

All the important men who were with him stared and stared, but they couldn't see any more than the others, although they responded just like the Emperor, "Oh, it is very beautiful!" And they advised him to dress in the new clothes for the first time in the Grand Procession that was to take place soon in the city. "They will be magnificent! Superb! Excellent!" it was passed from lip to lip. And with that, everybody was well satisfied. The Emperor gave each of the crooks a knight's medal and the title of Royal Loomsman.

The entire night before the procession, the swindlers sat up by the light of at least sixteen candles. The townsfolk could see they were busy finishing the Emperor's new clothes. The Swindlers pretended to take the cloth from the loom. They cut at the air with big scissors, and sewed away using needles without thread. At last they passed the words: "the clothes are ready."

The Emperor, with his best Court Chamberlains came straight away. The swindlers lifted their arms as though they were holding something, and said, "see, here are the trousers! Here is the jacket! Here is the cape!" and so forth. They are as light as a spider's web! One wouldn't believe one had anything on, but that is the virtue of it!"

"Oh quite! Yes, indeed!" said all the Court Chamberlains. But they could not see anything, for there was nothing to see.

"Would Your Royal Majesty now graciously be pleased to change your clothes?" said the swindlers. "Then we shall dress you in your new clothes over there by the big mirror."

The Emperor laid aside all his clothes, and the swindlers acted as if they dressed him in his new clothes. Finally, they pretended to wrap something around his waist which should have been the train; and the Emperor turned and spun around before the mirror.

20

"My goodness, how well they suit you! How nicely they fit! Such colours! It is an exquisite suit!" "They are waiting outside with the canopy which will be carried above Your Royal Majesty in the procession!" announced the Royal Master of Ceremonies. "Yes, well, I'm ready!" said the Emperor. "Don't my new clothes fit well?"

And then he turned again in front of the mirror, for he wanted everyone to believe he was admiring his finery. The Chamberlains who were to carry the train, fumbled with their hands along the floor, just as if they were taking up the train. They walked along holding the air, and dared not let anyone notice that they couldn't see anything.

21

And so the Emperor walked under the canopy in the procession, and all the people in the street and at the windows said: "Goodness, how grand the Emperor's new clothes are! What a lovely train! How well they fit him!" No one wanted anyone else to think that he could not see the clothes, for it would be thought that he was incompetent or that he was a fool. The Emperor's clothes had never before been such a success.

"But he is not wearing anything!" exclaimed a little child. "Listen to the voice of the innocent!" said his father; and one person whispered to the next repeating what the child had said.

"He isn't wearing anything. There is a child saying he isn't wearing anything!" "He isn't wearing anything!" shouted all the crowd at last. The Emperor trembled inside, for he felt himself that they may be right, but he thought, "I must go on and finish the procession." And so he held himself even more straight and proud, and the Chamberlains walked along carrying the train which wasn't even there.